i wish i was an Octopus

by Nigel Ward

For

Angus, Hamish, Charlotte,

Josie, Lachlan and Emily

I wish I was an Octopus

I've got so much to do

I'd have eight arms to do things with

Two arms is six too few!

If I was an Octopus

I'd zip through all my chores

I'd sweep and dust and scrub and mop

Without a single pause

If I was an Octopus

I could play lots of sports at once

Tennis, baseball, basketball

And other crazy stunts

If I was an Octopus

I'd play piano like a star

I'd even have a few spare arms

for cello and guitar

If I was an Octopus

No one could juggle as well as me

I'd spin eight balls high in the air

Too fast for you to see

If I was an Octopus

In the kitchen I'd be a master

I could chop and mix and bake and grill

And no-one would be faster

If I was an Octopus

Although I've got a lot to do

I'd have eight arms to get things done

To spend more time with you

If I was an Octopus

It really would be fun

I would give you lots of eight-armed hugs

and tickle everyone!

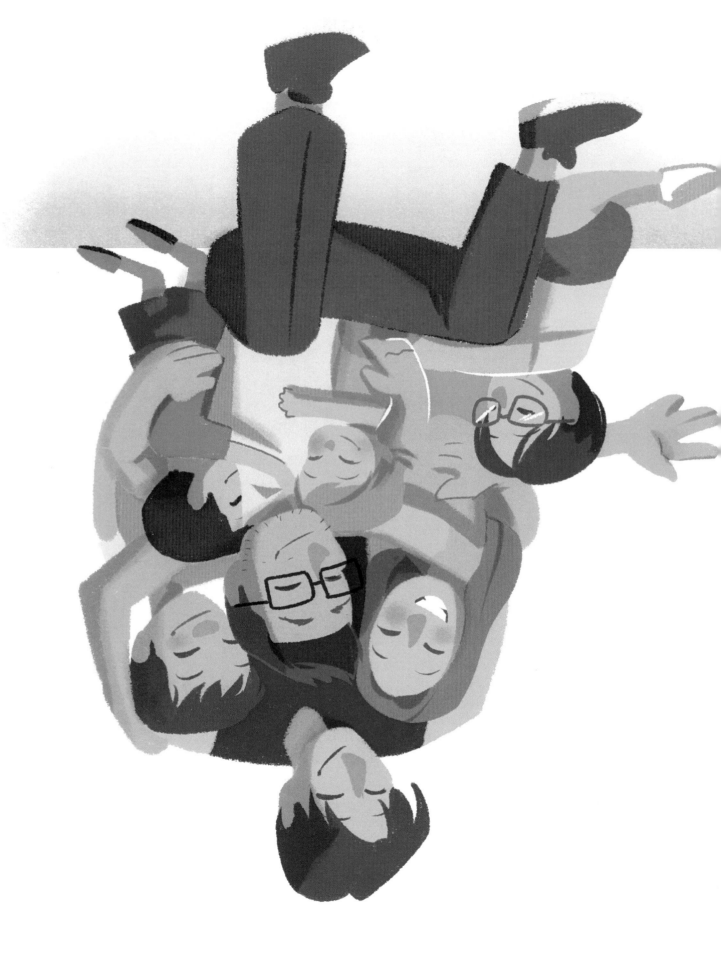

If you enjoyed this book
why not check out these books
by the same author

THERE'S A SHARK IN MY SHOWER!

By Nigel Ward

Illustrated by Nadica Zlatkova Mitevska

THERE'S A CROCODILE IN MY ATTIC!

By Nigel Ward

Illustrated by Nadica Zlatkova Mitevska

Made in United States
North Haven, CT
13 May 2022

19129121R00015